Artesian Press

MW01045085

TIMBER

SUSANNAH BRIN

Artesian Press
P.O. Box 355 Buena Park, CA 90621

Take Ten Books
Thrillers

Other Take Ten Themes:

Mystery
Sports
Adventure
Chillers
Fantasy
Disaster

Project Editor: Dwayne Epstein
Cover illustration : Fujiko
Graphic Design: Tony Amaro
©2001 Artesian Press

 *Artesian Press*

ISBN 1-58659-044-8

CONTENTS

Chapter 1

Jack Thompson neared the gate of Callahan's logging and sawmill camp. Before he saw the crowd, he heard their angry shouts. Frowning, he shifted his pickup into first gear and slowly inched it forward.

When someone kicked his truck, Jack braked and glanced in his rearview mirror. He didn't see anyone. Whoever had banged on his bumper had quickly slipped back into the mob of shouting protesters.

While he was stopped, a pretty blond woman knocked on his window. "Save the trees! Don't cut them down," pleaded the young woman.

Jack smiled at the girl. "My first day as a logger and you're asking me to quit before I even get started?"

"Did you know that some of the trees you'll be cutting down are more than five hundred years old? And those trees are home to hundreds of animals," she went on earnestly.

Jack laughed. "Maybe we could talk about this when I get off work." He stepped on the gas pedal and revved the engine.

The young woman stared at him for several seconds, then walked away.

Jack drove on into the camp. It wasn't much different from the one he had worked at during the summer after high school. *Of course there weren't protesters blocking the gates three years ago,* thought Jack. Then, seeing what he was looking for, he parked in front of a trailer marked *Office.*

A semi-flatbed truck loaded with milled lumber rumbled past, kicking up clouds of dust. Jack hadn't taken more than a few steps when he heard a familiar voice call his name. Turning, he saw his old friend, Tim Callahan. *Tim hasn't changed,* thought Jack. *He's still as thin as a beanpole and bristling with nervous energy.*

"It's good to see you, buddy," said Jack, giving Tim Callahan a friendly slap on the back.

"You, too, Jack. It's been a long time. I heard you were back," said Tim.

"I ran into your Uncle Harry up in Portland. He said there would be a job waiting for me any time I wanted to work. So here I am."

At the mention of his uncle, Tim frowned. "Yeah, he told me," said Tim, staring hard at the door of the trailer.

Jack followed Tim's eyes. "I'm sorry about your dad, Tim. He was really a great guy."

A pained expression clouded Tim's face. "Thanks. He died in his sleep. A heart attack," said Tim. Clearing his throat, he went on. "Uncle Harry has the controlling interest in the company now. That makes me what you'd call a junior partner."

"Then I guess I should be asking *you* if I have a job," said Jack, trying to lighten up his friend's mood.

"Yeah? If it was up to me, you'd still be looking for a job," joked Tim, his eyes dancing with amusement.

Knowing that Tim was teasing him, Jack played along. "Is that so? What about all those favors I did for you when we were in high school?"

"What favors were those?" asked Tim, pretending ignorance.

"How about all those dates I lined up for you?"

Tim smiled. "Okay, so I was shy back then. I've gotten over it."

Jack laughed. "Speaking of dates, do you know that cute blond girl down by the gate?"

Tim's mouth tightened into a hard line. "Katie Morrison. She works up at

Bowers' Lodge. I hate to tell you this, Jack, but she's bad news"

Before Jack could ask more about Katie Morrison, the blast of a sharp siren split the air. The door to the office flew open and Harry Callahan, Tim's uncle, stepped out. Dressed in freshly pressed business clothes and wearing thick glasses, Harry Callahan looked like what he was—an accountant. For years, his brother had run the logging operation. Harry had been in charge of sales and accounting. "What's wrong now?" Harry asked impatiently.

"The mill!" Tim yelled over his shoulder as he ran toward the mill.

Harry quickly greeted Jack, and then they hurried after Tim.

The inside of the mill was quiet. The trunk of a giant Douglas fir lay like a fallen soldier on the carriage bed. Hanging motionless above the log was a huge saw. Its blades were bent and twisted.

"Not *again!*" moaned Harry, turning to the mill foreman Ron Bueller.

"Third spike this week," said Ron, pointing to the iron wedge that had been driven deep into the tree trunk.

"Looks like we'll have to inspect every log before we start sawing," said Tim after studying the wedge.

"That would take an awful lot of extra time," Ron said, glancing from Tim to Harry.

"Way too much time," Harry said sternly. "We're already behind on this week's shipment."

"If the blade hits one of these spikes at the wrong angle, it could explode. Someone could get hurt," argued Tim.

Harry Callahan nodded. "I know, Tim. I don't want anyone to get hurt, either. But we've got deadlines to meet." Harry turned to leave. "I think that it's high time I had a talk with the protesters."

"Ha! You know you can't reason

with those tree-huggers," Tim snorted.

Harry fixed his eyes on his nephew. "Do you have a better idea?"

"Yeah. I say we get a few of the other loggers. Then we go down there and pound some sense into them."

Annoyed, Harry threw up his hands in frustration. "That will certainly do a lot of good," he said sarcastically.

"Are you *sure* it's a protester who's driving the wedges into the logs?" asked Jack, trying to ease the tension between the two men.

"Of course it's one of those tree-huggers," snapped Tim.

"Have you notified the police?" Jack asked in a worried voice.

"I talked to the sheriff. He said he couldn't do anything. Not without some proof," said Harry.

"Then why don't you hire a private investigator?" Jack asked.

"Hmmm. A private investigator. I wonder how much they charge." Harry mumbled, thinking out loud.

Tim frowned and kicked at the rocks in the dirt as they turned toward the office. "Weren't you in the military police when you were in the army, Jack?" asked Tim.

"Yes, I was," Jack replied.

"Well then, we don't need to hire anyone," said Tim, looking cheerful again. "*You* could help us to catch whoever's sabotaging our operation."

Jack didn't know what to say. Sure, he'd been in the military police. But that didn't mean he knew anything about being a detective. Most of his work had been routine arrests of GIs who'd gone AWOL or had too much to drink. The one time he tried to figure out who had been stealing from the commissary, he'd blown the case and his partner had gotten hurt. No, he wasn't going to play detective again. The stakes were too high. "Hire a professional. I don't think I'd be much help. Besides, I signed on to work as a logger—remember?" said Jack, avoiding his friend's eyes.

"But it's going to take a while to hire someone else, and *you're* already here. You would really be helping us out, Jack," said Harry.

"I'm sorry. This kind of thing is out of my league," said Jack.

Harry nodded. "Okay. Well, I'll call up to Portland then. There's got to be somebody up there who can help us."

Jack watched as the older man disappeared into the office. Glancing at Tim, he felt a pang of guilt. His friend looked worried.

Even though Tim smiled and acted like it was no big deal, Jack couldn't shake the feeling that somehow he had let the Callahans down.

Chapter 2

The sun had just started to come up when Jack entered the mess hall. The smell of fresh coffee and bacon made his stomach growl. Grabbing a tray, he joined a line of men waiting for breakfast. In front of him, a short, wiry man in a red shirt joked with a couple of loggers seated at a nearby table.

"Why, just last year I topped a tree taller than a forty-story building," bragged the small man.

"Maybe so, Smitty, but I bet it took you all day just to climb to the top," teased a big-bellied logger.

"I got there faster than you can fork in those pancakes," shot back the wiry little tree-topper.

"Then you haven't seen how fast old Jake here can shovel it in," joked another logger. The other men laughed along, then went back to eating.

The man in front of Jack turned around. "Smitty Macallister," he said, extending his hand.

Jack shook the man's hand and introduced himself.

"Haven't seen you around. You ever log before?" asked Smitty.

"Yes. I spent a summer working for Tim's dad. But that was a few years ago," explained Jack.

Smitty nodded and stepped forward in line. "Tim's dad was a good man— a good logger. He would have known how to deal with these protesters." Smitty stepped forward, pushing his tray toward the cook, a grumpy-looking man with one arm. "Jack, meet Lou Williams, the worst cook this side of the Rockies," teased Smitty.

Lou Williams glared at Smitty, then slapped a plate heaped with bacon and eggs onto Smitty's tray. "Move on. You're holding up the line, superstar," the cook snarled.

Jack smiled at the cook as he reached for his plate of eggs. But Lou Williams only grunted in reply, then waved his spatula at Jack, signaling him to move on.

Following Smitty to a table, Jack overheard two loggers talking about the protesters.

"They complain about us all day, then at night they go home to their houses built of wood. I bet not one of them thinks about saving a tree when they're at the lumberyard buying boards to build a deck or a new fence!"

"What really burns me is when they call me a 'timber beast'—like I'm out there destroying the forests. Why, I love the woods just as much as the next man!" cried Smitty.

Jack could hear the frustration and anger in the men's voices."

We could run those protesters out of here," said one of the loggers.

"How?" asked Jack, even though he had a pretty good idea what the man was going to say.

"Scare them off. Ten of us with chainsaws should do the trick."

"Won't do any good," said Tim, pulling up a chair. "John Bowers will just hire more people just like them to take their place."

Jack smiled at his friend. He was glad to see him.

"You think John Bowers is behind what's been happening?" asked Smitty, his mouth stuffed with food.

Tim sipped his coffee, then said, "He's got the money and the power in this area. He's worried that when the rains come, loose dirt will wash down the mountain and into the river. His rich fishermen clients don't want to fish in a muddy river, you know."

"Yeah, but you're doing *selective* logging," said Jack. "It's not like you're stripping all the vegetation."

"I know, but there's no reasoning with the man." Tim stood up. "Smitty, you and Jack meet me at the office. Harry wants us to top a tree up on the north face. We're going to cable log that whole area."

Jack noticed how surprised Smitty looked. "I thought we were going to lift the logs out of there with helium-filled balloons," Smitty said in surprise.

"Harry vetoed the idea. He said it would cost too much." Tim shrugged, indicating that the matter was beyond his control.

Jack gulped the last of his coffee and followed Smitty and Tim to the pickup. As the truck bumped up the hill, Tim explained to Jack that they had a contract with the Forest Service to log ten acres on the north slope and another fifteen acres to the south.

"Sure is pretty up here," said Jack, admiring a stand of 500-year-old trees.

"You turning into a tree-hugger too?" snorted Smitty, parking the truck on the side of a newly bulldozed road.

"No, but I can understand why they're protesting," said Jack.

"We *all* can!" snapped Tim. "That's why we agreed to selective cutting and replanting. That's why we signed a 250-page contract that spells out what we can and can't do."

Smitty selected a tree to use as a cable pole, while Tim explained the contract. "For every acre we log, we have to leave three logs on the ground to keep the animals happy. We've even agreed to wire habitat logs across the streams."

"That's a good one," grunted Smitty. "Used to be it was a violation to leave a log lying across a stream or river."

"Wow, things have really changed,"

said Jack, realizing how much had happened in the past three years.

"And not for the better," grumbled Tim as he pulled metal leg harnesses from the equipment pile.

"How about it, Tim? You want to top this baby?" asked Smitty.

Tim studied the 300-foot tree. "I can't. Uncle Harry doesn't believe in partners climbing trees," he complained.

Smitty gave Tim a sympathetic look and then he strapped the metal harnesses to his own legs. Spikes on the insides of the leg harnesses would help grip the tree. Using a guide rope that circled both his waist and the tree, Smitty began climbing the huge fir.

"*I* should be topping this tree," Tim grumbled to Jack, his eyes following Smitty's progress.

"Why would you want to? Looks dangerous to me," said Jack, trying to cheer up his friend.

"My dad did it when he was young.

He and Lou Williams used to top trees for the Union Pacific."

"Lou, the cook?" asked Jack.

"Yeah, he and my dad started out together."

Jack craned his neck skyward. *Topping a tree*, he thought to himself, *would be about the* last *thing I would ever want to do!*

"*I* should be running this camp, Jack. Not Harry. He knows accounts and sales, but he doesn't know the first thing about how to run a logging camp. He's always—"

Tim's attention was suddenly on Smitty. Something was wrong. Smitty's body no longer hugged the huge trunk of the tree. The man was falling. The ends of the guide rope fluttered like ribbons around Smitty's waist as he plummeted toward the ground.

Chapter 3

Jack could still hear the siren of the ambulance as it sped toward the county hospital, carrying Smitty's broken body. It was quiet down by the gate. The few protesters who'd shown up earlier in the day were gone. He glanced at the broken guide rope in his hand. Everyone had been told that Smitty's fall was an accident—that his rope had snapped. Jack wasn't so sure.

"Jack, could we talk to you?" asked Harry.

"Sure thing." Jack thought the older man looked as though he'd aged ten years in the last few hours.

The mess hall was deserted except for Lou Williams, who stood by the sink peeling potatoes. Jack dropped the rope on the table.

"Do *you* think it was an accident, Jack?" asked Harry.

"It's happened before," said Tim.

"Recently?" Jack asked.

"Years ago. Dad told me about a rope breaking on a guy when they were logging down in Tillamook," Tim said, fingering the rope.

"So these things *do* happen?" said Harry, shaking his head sadly.

Jack wanted to put Harry's mind at rest. But he wasn't sure that it was a freak accident. "It looks cut," said Jack, pointing to the straight threads of the break. "I could be wrong, but . . ."

Harry wrung his hands and said, "I don't know how a protester could have gotten hold of the rope. All of the equipment is locked up at night."

"Maybe it wasn't a protester who cut the rope," suggested Jack.

Tim laughed harshly. "Who else could it be? You can't honestly believe that a logger or mill worker would do something like this!"

"Stranger things have happened," shrugged Jack. He remembered the time he'd caught a drill sergeant stealing from recruits and putting them on report.

Harry took off his glasses and wiped them with a handkerchief. "What are we going to do?"

"We could shut down for a few days," said Tim. "At least until we find out who's sabotaging the camp."

Harry put his glasses on and looked hard at his nephew. "We're already behind schedule. Profits are down from last year and—"

Tim stood up and kicked his chair into a nearby table. "*Numbers!* That's all you care about. What if someone else gets hurt?" he yelled angrily.

Harry studied a stain on the table. When he spoke, his voice shook. "Running a company is about profit and loss. And right now, this company is financially hurting."

"Have it your way—but if anyone else gets hurt it's going to be on your head," hissed Tim. He turned and stomped out of the mess hall.

Jack turned to Harry. "Did you find a private investigator?"

Harry shook his head. "I called up to Portland, but no one's available right now. I'm going to keep trying."

Jack watched Harry leave the mess hall. He felt sorry for the older man. He carried his coffee cup over to the counter. "Tim said you had logged with his dad," said Jack.

"Yup," said Lou, staring at Jack.

"Do *you* think someone is trying to sabotage the company?" asked Jack.

"Maybe. Or maybe this company

has just simply run out of luck."

Jack smiled to himself. He didn't believe in luck. He thought a person made his own luck. "Luck?"

"Back in '48 I was living good," Lou said. "I was making a hundred dollars a day. Then one day, my luck run out. I lost my arm. Some said I was lucky to be alive. I guess it depends on how you look at it." Then he turned on the faucet and began filling a pot with water, ending their conversation.

As Jack left the mess hall, he thought about Lou Williams. How had the cook lost his arm? Realizing that he was starting to play detective, Jack pushed all thoughts of the one-armed cook from his mind.

A pickup slowed, then stopped. "Get in. We're going to finish what Smitty started this morning," yelled Tim.

"Who's going to top the tree?" Jack asked as he climbed into the pickup.

"I am," said Tim.

Surprised, Jack turned and stared at his friend. "I thought your uncle said no climbing for partners."

"He doesn't have a choice now." Tim pressed down on the gas, and the pickup shot forward up the dirt road.

"So you get your wish after all," said Jack.

Tim eyed him coldly. "What are you talking about?"

"This morning you were upset about not topping the tree, that's all," said Jack.

When they reached the site, Tim grabbed the equipment and headed into the woods. After strapping on the leg harnesses and inspecting the new guide rope, he started climbing the giant Douglas fir.

By the time Tim reached the top, Jack had stopped worrying. Everything was running smoothly. Suddenly, the word *Timber!* echoed through the quiet forest. Jack jumped as the treetop crashed to the ground a few feet from where he had been standing.

Glancing back up the tree, he saw Tim climbing up on the fresh cut. *He's going to dance a jig,* thought Jack, feeling a sudden rush of fear. If Tim fell, Jack knew they wouldn't need an ambulance. They would need a coffin. He held his breath as Tim shrieked like an Indian and danced for a couple of minutes before making his way back down the tree. On the ground, he unsnapped his guide rope and turned to Jack. "Want to try it?" asked Tim, his eyes sparkling.

"No."

"You get a real birdseye view of the valley from up there," said Tim, high with excitement.

"Yeah? If they put your brain in a bird, I'd guarantee that it would fly backwards," said Jack, a little disgusted. "That was a foolhardy stunt you just pulled up there. You could have fallen." He picked up the chainsaw and headed for the truck.

Tim grabbed his gear and followed. "You don't understand. I've wanted to do that since I was a kid. I just wish Dad was here to see me."

"Your dancing hasn't improved," said Jack, still bugged that Tim had given him such a scare.

Tim laughed. "Remember the prom? You forced me to get up and dance. And somehow my foot got tangled in Mary's dress and—"

"And you ripped her skirt half off," laughed Jack. Remembering, they both laughed until their sides ached.

By the time they reached the bottom of the mountain, they had talked about old times and caught up on what they had both been doing the past three years. Jack was glad that Tim had lost some of his earlier moodiness. "Why don't we go over to Bowers' Lodge for dinner tonight? Celebrate our reunion," suggested Jack.

Tim frowned. "Whose side are you on, anyway?"

"What does that mean?"

"You refuse to help us find out who is sabotaging the camp. And now you want to party with the enemy," spat Tim. He got out of the truck and slammed the door.

"I thought we could snoop around," Jack said. "Maybe we'll hear something. Like the time we sneaked into the other team's locker room and stole all of their plays."

"We're not in high school anymore, Jack!" snapped Tim. Without another word, he stormed off in the direction of his trailer.

Chapter 4

The pickup's headlights slashed through the black night as Jack drove toward Bowers' Lodge. He was still thinking about Tim. Why had he been acting so strangely—happy one minute and angry the next? It was like his friend had become two people. There was the Tim Jack knew and loved—and then there was this cold and angry person he didn't know.

Jack realized that Tim had been through an awful lot. He'd lost his dad, become a partner in the company, and now he had to deal with the protesters. *And to make matters worse,* thought Jack, *I refused to help him find out who is sabotaging the camp. He probably thinks I'm the one who's changed into someone else.*

Then Jack remembered Katie Morrison. He thought about what she had said about the forest being home to hundreds of animals. She and the other protesters were right—something had to be done to save the forests. But the loggers were just doing their job. They gave the public the lumber it needed. Somehow the two groups were going to have to learn to work together, to find a balance.

Seeing a large sign that said *Bowers' Lodge,* Jack turned left and followed the road into a wide parking lot. As he parked, he watched as a man drove off, getting a glimpse of his face. It was the camp cook, Lou Williams! *What is Lou Williams doing at Bowers' Lodge?* Jack wondered.

Crossing to the entrance of the lodge, Jack passed several couples. Overhearing their conversation, he guessed that a meeting of the Save The

Trees committee had just broken up.

The interior of the lodge was warm and cozy. The lobby opened into an even larger room with a massive, free-standing fireplace made of river rock. Sofas, chairs, and tables had been placed on both sides of the fireplace and along the wall of windows that overlooked the river. Jack plopped himself down into an overstuffed chair that faced the fireplace. From where he sat, he had a view of the lobby and the room on the other side of the fireplace. He glanced around. Behind him, Katie Morrison and a waiter were busy clearing dirty dishes from the tables.

Jack leaned toward the fire and waited for her to come over.

"Could I get you something?" asked Katie.

Jack stared at the fire. "A beer and a piece of berry pie."

"Ugh, what a combination," she laughed, making a face.

Jack watched Katie as she walked toward the kitchen. He remembered Tim's warning about Katie being "bad news." From where he sat, she looked like nothing but good news.

Looking across the hearth and through the opening of the fireplace, Jack could see two middle-aged men sitting at a table in the other room. One man was dressed in a business suit, and the other wore slacks and a sweater. From their faces, Jack guessed that the men were arguing about something. He leaned closer to the fireplace, hoping to catch some of their conversation.

"Your pie and beer," said Katie, placing his order on the table.

"Thanks," said Jack. "I guess I missed the meeting," he went on, fishing for information.

"You mean the Save The Trees meeting?" asked Katie.

"Yeah."

"It broke up a few minutes ago."

"Darn," said Jack. "I was hoping to hear what you plan to do next."

"Well, we're going to continue demonstrating. And, you know, just try and hassle them as much as possible," said Katie, wiping a nearby table.

"Does that include sabotaging equipment?" asked Jack.

Katie turned and stared at him. Surprise and recognition dawned on her face. "So *that's* why you looked familiar. I saw you at the camp."

Jack smiled. "Right. You tried to convince me to quit my job. I said we'd discuss it later. Well, here I am."

Katie glanced around nervously. "You shouldn't have come here. John Bowers is sitting just on the other side of this fireplace," whispered Katie.

"So?"

"We aren't ever supposed to serve anyone from the logging company."

Katie's eyes were wide with fear.

She reminded him of a frightened deer.

"Calm down. He doesn't know me. Besides, I can take care of myself," said Jack with a smile.

Katie smiled weakly, then glanced around the room. "I have to get back to work." She started to leave.

"Was cutting Smitty's rope just another way to hassle us?" asked Jack.

He saw a look of shock cross her face. "I didn't . . . I mean, we didn't have anything to do with that! We're protesters, not terrorists. Do you really think it *wasn't* an accident?"

"I don't really know. Tim thinks a protester may have cut the rope."

Katie frowned and stared at the fire for several seconds. "I wouldn't believe everything Tim says."

"Why not?" asked Jack.

Katie glanced at Jack, then down at the floor. Nervously, her fingers played with the hem of her apron. "He only sees what he wants to see. He's got a chip on his shoulder, and yet . . . it's more than that . . ."

"The protesters haven't exactly made his life easy," said Jack, trying to defend his friend.

"It's not just that. He's—" The two men who'd been sitting in the other room had walked into the lobby. "Oh, here comes Mr. Bowers and his lawyer friend," said Katie.

"Which one is Bowers?" asked Jack, studying the two men.

Katie nodded her head, indicating the tall, handsome man dressed in slacks and a sweater. "I have to go." Carrying a tray of dishes, she hurried from the room.

Jack dropped a five-dollar bill on the table and strolled into the lobby. Standing by the door, John Bowers argued softly with his lawyer. Jack heard enough to realize that Tim was right—Bowers' Lodge was surely enemy territory.

Chapter 5

It was after midnight when Jack pulled into camp. He was tired. It had been a long day and an even longer night. The camp was dark except for the tiny pools of light spilling down from the utility bulbs that were strung along the road.

As he walked across the road, Jack heard voices. Not wanting to be seen, he slipped between two trailers and waited. As the voices drew nearer, Jack tiptoed around the front of the trailer and made his way up the hill. He hadn't gone very far when two men appeared. Ducking back between the trailers, Jack stared hard through the darkness, hoping to catch a glimpse of the men's faces. But it was too dark.

After the men had passed, Jack slid out from between the trailers and followed. He heard one of the men chuckle and then disappear into the darkness near the mess hall. As Jack started to cross the road, the other man turned and started walking back in Jack's direction. Quickly, Jack stepped back, but his leg hit a trailer hitch, throwing him off balance. He crashed into the trailer, and then suddenly he felt someone on top of him. Twisting and kicking, the two men rolled out into the road. Jack tasted dirt. His face felt like a shovel digging into the stony ground.

Finally, gathering all of his strength into one quick movement, Jack flipped the man off his back. As the other man started to get up, Jack grabbed his leg, pulling him back down to the ground. Punching wildly at the man, Jack hit him in the stomach, making him curl up into a ball. As Jack staggered to his feet, he got a good look at the other man's face.

"Tim?" It was his friend!

Tim groaned and clutched his stomach.

Jack knelt down and carefully helped his friend to his feet. "Why did you jump me?"

"I thought you were a protester," Tim mumbled, straightening up and rubbing his stomach. "What were you doing sneaking around in the dark?"

"I was on my way to the trailer when I heard voices. I thought you and that other guy were trying to sabotage the camp," said Jack.

Tim gave a weak laugh. "What an imagination! I couldn't sleep, so I took a walk. Then I ran into Lou Williams down by the loading deck. *Ouch!* I think you knocked my stomach into my backbone."

"You weren't doing all that bad yourself," said Jack, spitting out dirt.

They looked at each other and broke out laughing.

Suddenly, lights went on in the trailer behind them. Harry Callahan stepped out into the night air, wearing a flannel nightshirt and carrying a shotgun. "Who's there?" cried Harry in a frightened voice.

"Don't shoot! It's just me and Jack," cried Tim.

Harry lowered the shotgun and squinted at them. "What's going on?"

"Nothing . . ." Jack glanced at Tim and started laughing again. For some reason the whole episode reminded him of a Three Stooges movie.

"Go to bed before you wake up the whole camp!" Harry snorted. He went back into his trailer.

Still laughing, Jack and Tim started walking toward their trailers. Neither spoke for several seconds. Finally, Tim broke the awkward silence. "About what happened earlier tonight . . ."

"Forget it," said Jack.

"I don't know why I got so angry. Lately, I just—"

"I said forget it," said Jack. "You were right about Bowers. He really hates loggers."

"I *told* you," Tim said defensively.

"Tonight I overheard him talking to a lawyer. I don't know what it is he's planning, but he's up to something."

"He's probably paying one of those tree-huggers to sabotage the company," said Tim.

"I don't know. Katie Morrison doesn't think—"

"I told you to stay clear of her."

Jack was surprised by the sudden anger he heard in Tim's voice. Then a thought crossed his mind. He grinned. "Tell me, do you have a crush on her or something?" asked Jack.

"No. I took her out a few times when we first got here—but we didn't hit it off." Tim opened the door to his trailer. "I gathered as much," said Jack, grinning.

"Why? What did she say about me?" asked Tim, staring hard at Jack.

"Nothing, really—except that you have a chip on your shoulder."

"She's crazy," said Tim.

"I think you still like her, buddy," teased Jack.

"If you think that, you're as crazy as she is," snapped Tim. "Just forget about her. We've got to find out what Bowers is up to."

"Let's leave that to whoever your uncle hires," said Jack.

Tim frowned. "Oh, I forgot. You don't want to get involved. So why don't you quit sticking your nose in it, man?" With an angry snort, Tim walked off.

Chapter 6

When Jack stepped out of his trailer the next morning, he found himself surrounded by cold, damp fog. He shivered and buttoned his jacket.

"Let's go!" yelled Tim, leaning out the window of the pickup.

"I haven't even had breakfast yet," complained Jack as he swung up into the cab of the truck.

Tim shifted and stepped on the gas. "Here," he said, handing Jack some coffee and a bag of sandwiches.

"Thanks. You're a real pal." Jack poured himself a cup of coffee and took a big bite of an egg sandwich. Glancing up, he saw that his friend looked tense and uptight. "So what are we doing today?"

Tim scowled. "Setting chokes. We were supposed to cut trees on the south slope, but Harry changed the schedule."

Jack laughed. "I thought we did that last night."

"What?" mumbled Tim.

"Never mind," said Jack, realizing that Tim wasn't getting the joke.

"It really bugs me the way Harry changes the work assignments. He *thinks* he knows what he's doing, but he doesn't know anything," fumed Tim.

"Why are you getting so upset?" asked Jack. "Wrapping chains around logs can't be that difficult."

"It isn't, but it's dangerous."

"Not as dangerous as topping trees and dancing on the fresh cut," said Jack, puzzled by Tim's sudden concern with safety.

"You're right," Tim said wearily. "I guess I'm just tired. This is how it works. After chaining the log, we attach the chain to the skyline cable. Then we signal down to the loading deck to start the skyline. The computer has been programmed with a four-minute lag time. It activates the system exactly four minutes after we signal."

"I get it. We have four minutes to run for cover," said Jack.

They worked steadily through the morning without a break. By noon, Jack was tired. Setting chokes was hard, dirty work. As he followed Tim away from the log they'd just chained, he heard a groaning sound. Glancing back, he saw that the log was starting to lift off the ground. Seeing that he was too close, he ran to the clearing where Tim stood talking on the walkie-talkie.

"Didn't you hear me tell you to take cover?" shouted Tim.

"Yeah. I guess I'm getting a little tired," said Jack. The skyline cables yanked the giant log higher into the air.

"If that baby fell on you, you'd be flatter than a pancake," warned Tim, watching the giant fir fly down the mountain on the skyline.

"Quit worrying! I had plenty of time."

"That's probably what Lou Williams thought the day he lost his arm," said Tim. "He and my dad had just finished setting the choke when someone started the skyline. They ran for cover, but Lou was too slow. A loose limb fell and ripped off his arm."

Jack's stomach flipflopped. He swallowed, then took a deep breath. "Why did the man below start the skyline moving?"

"I don't know. Maybe he thought he saw my dad signal. They used hand signals in those days." Tim picked up his equipment and walked toward another felled tree.

"I'm surprised Lou didn't quit the logging business all together," said Jack.

"He did. Then about two years ago, he showed up and asked for a cooking job. Dad was real pleased to see him again. I think he had always felt guilty about what happened to Lou."

"Do you think Lou holds your dad responsible?" asked Jack.

"Naw. Lou loved my dad. He cried like a baby at the funeral. He's a funny old guy, but I dig him. He's family."

When Tim talked so fondly about the cook, Jack saw his face relax. He decided not to tell him that he'd seen the cook leaving Bowers' Lodge.

"Why don't you start up at that end of the log," said Tim, pointing toward the uphill section of the tree. "Try to cut off as many limbs as possible."

"Sure."

"And this time when I call *clear*, get the heck out of there," yelled Tim, dragging a chain across the huge log.

"Quit worrying—I can run a mile in four minutes," joked Jack.

"I don't remember you setting any track records in school," grumbled Tim.

Amused, Jack shook his head. Tim was acting like a mother hen. Working quickly, he attached the choke chain around the log. Then he picked up his chainsaw and started hacking off the limbs that hadn't fallen off when the tree was cut down. He'd cut about four big limbs when he happened to glance up and see Tim signaling for him to get down. "Okay!" he yelled. He started to jump off the log, then remembered that he'd left his jacket farther up.

Suddenly, Jack felt the giant log move beneath his feet. Something was wrong. Overhead the cables whined. Without looking, he jumped, hitting the ground just as a giant limb whipped toward him. Out of the corner of his eye, he saw Tim running toward him.

"Jack!" screamed Tim.

Suddenly the giant log twisted. The trunk swung to the right, knocking Tim to the ground.

Chapter 7

Jack leaned against the side of the first-aid trailer. The swinging log hadn't hurt Tim, but he'd gotten a nasty cut on his cheek when he'd hit the ground. Jack tried not to think about what would have happened if the log had hit Tim much harder.

The door to the first-aid trailer opened and Harry Callahan stepped out. "He has a headache, but that cut on his face is just a scratch. Thank God he's okay. I would never forgive myself if something had happened to him. Especially after the fuss he made this morning. He sure didn't want to set chokes," said Harry, frowning sadly. "But then he makes a fuss about *everything* I do or say."

"It's my fault," Jack said. "I knew he'd signaled the computer. I should have gotten off, but I went back for my jacket. I thought I had more time."

Harry patted Jack on the shoulder. "Don't blame yourself. Four minutes can go by pretty fast."

Jack looked thoughtfully at Harry. "Maybe I *didn't* have four minutes," he said, suddenly suspicious.

"Of course you did. The lag time is regulated by the computer's clock."

"I know, but what if someone changed it?" said Jack, thinking aloud. "Where is the control box?"

"It's attached to the steel tower," said Harry, pointing toward a tall metal structure near the loading deck.

Jack and Harry headed up the hill. "The control box is locked, Jack. And I have the only key right here," said Harry, reaching into his pocket and pulling out a padlock key.

"I want to look at it anyway," said

Jack. He stopped at the top of the hill and watched as a giant log was tossed off the skyline onto the deck. The earth trembled. After the log had settled, Jack raced across the deck to the metal tower. Quickly, he climbed up the rigging to the metal box that controlled the skyline. "Wait, Jack. You'll need this," yelled Harry, waving the key.

Jack shook his head. He didn't need the key. The padlock was gone. He lifted the lid. The clock on the tiny computer control read two minutes. He took a small knife from his pocket and reset the lag time to four minutes.

"Someone pried the padlock off the box and reset the clock," said Jack, as he jumped from the rigging. Now he was angry. Angry at whoever had changed the clock, and angry at himself for not getting involved sooner. "You and Tim were right. Someone *is* trying to put you out of business. And whoever it is doesn't give a darn about who gets hurt."

Harry stared at the sky, then down at his hands. He shook his head sadly. "I thought this really was an accident. I've tried to ignore the problem. Now I can't—there are too many accidents." He started walking down the hill.

"What are you going to do?"

Harry threw up his hands. "Close the camp until I can hire someone to get to the bottom of all of this!"

"But you can't afford to shut down," argued Jack, remembering what Harry had said a few days earlier.

"I don't have a choice." Harry took off his glasses and rubbed his eyes.

"Wait. Let's go over everything that's happened," said Jack, trying to fit the puzzle pieces together in his mind.

Harry put his glasses back on and gazed at Jack hopefully.

"If you shut down, we'll never find

out who is sabotaging the camp."

"Maybe not. But at least no one else will get hurt," said Harry.

"I don't think there will be anymore accidents today. So far, the pattern has been one accident per day, right?" said Jack, his mind spinning with ideas.

Harry frowned. "Meaning we can count on another accident tomorrow?"

"Not if we can catch the creep," said Jack in a determined voice.

"And just how are we going to do that?" asked Harry.

Jack smiled. "We'll set a trap."

Chapter 8

The fog lifted that night, and the air turned clear and cold. Jack didn't notice the drop in temperature. Like a soldier ready for battle, his body was on alert.

He rattled the door handle on the maintenance trailer, but it was locked. After making certain that the coast was clear, he knocked lightly on the trailer window. Two taps from inside told him what he needed to know. Jack imagined Harry Callahan hunkered down by the window, an iron crowbar in his hand.

They're all in position, he thought. Ron Bueller was hidden in the mill, and Tim was covering the loading deck. *Whoever is sabotaging the camp is in for a little surprise tonight*, Jack thought to himself. *Yes sir, a little surprise.*

Sliding away from the maintenance trailer, Jack made his way up the hill toward a giant pile of logs. He had asked Harry to announce at dinner that the company would not do any logging the next day. Everyone would help to get out a special order. Harry told them that the rush job was the only thing that would keep the company from going under. Jack grinned, recalling Harry's speech. The old guy had given a very convincing performance.

Jack whistled softly. When no one answered, he whistled again. But again, he heard only silence. I hope he didn't fall asleep, thought Jack, as he circled around to where Tim was supposed to be. "Tim!" whispered Jack, in a low, hissing voice. But Tim wasn't there. "Shoot, I told him to sit tight," Jack muttered under his breath. He hoped his friend hadn't decided to play detective on his own.

Checking to see that the coast was clear, Jack peered into the darkness. Nothing moved. He darted across the loading deck and dropped down into a pile of sawdust. Skirting the main entrance of the mill, he slid along the side of the building to the pond. The back of the mill looked liked a giant black mouth, a dark cave. Quietly, Jack pulled himself up onto the catwalk that ran the length of the mill.

Moonlight bounced off the giant sawblade that hung from the ceiling. The sharp metal teeth of the big saw winked in the moonbeams, looking threatening and deadly.

Jack whistled softly to signal Ron Bueller. When there was no answer, Jack tensed. Something was wrong. Quietly, he crept along the catwalk. Then he heard someone moan. Jack froze. He stared into the darkness but couldn't see anyone. Then he heard the moan again. It seemed to be coming from the other side of the giant log that lay in the middle of the carriage. Without thinking, Jack jumped from the catwalk to the log below. Landing off balance, he slipped and fell spread-eagled on the barkless fir. Then once again, he heard someone moan. "Ron, is that you?" he whispered.

Suddenly the huge saw roared to life, loud and terrifying. Its teeth ripped through the wood like a knife slicing butter. Jack stood up on the log and ran away from the approaching blade. He glanced down at the carriage bed. For a moment Jack thought about jumping. But he knew that if he landed wrong, his legs would be caught in the gears. Imagining the gears grinding his legs to powder, he shuddered.

Jack looked back up at the catwalk. It didn't take him long to see that it was too high—he couldn't reach it. There was nothing he could do but keep running toward the mouth of the mill.

Suddenly Jack froze. A dark figure stood at the end of the log, blocking his exit. In the moonlight, Jack could see the dark figure strike a match that flickered, then died. Behind him, Jack heard the big saw grinding closer and closer.

The man lit another match and tossed it into the darkness. Again, the match flickered and died. Suddenly it occurred to Jack that the man was trying to set the mill on fire!

No matter what, Jack couldn't let that happen. If the mill caught fire, all that dry wood would burn in a flash. And somewhere behind him in the darkness, Ron Bueller lay hurt.

Lowering his head, Jack charged forward like a defensive tackle. He plowed into the man, sweeping him back off of the log and into the ice-cold pond water below.

Chapter 9

Outside the mess hall, Jack could see the flashing red light of the sheriff's car. Like gawkers at an accident scene, several loggers stood nearby watching to see what was happening. Behind him, Jack heard Harry talking quietly with the sheriff. Ron Bueller sat at Jack's right, drinking coffee and holding his head. Except for the nasty bump on his head where he'd been hit, Ron seemed to be all right.

Wearily, Jack ran his hand through his wet hair. He tried not to look at the handcuffed figure huddled in a blanket by the door. The whole thing seemed like a bad dream. Taking a deep breath, he got up and walked toward his sad-looking friend. *"Why?"* asked Jack, his voice shaking with emotion.

Tim looked up and smiled. It was the strange smile of someone gone out of his mind. "Hey, good buddy, you been swimming?"

Shivering, Jack pulled the blanket tighter around his shoulders. "We've both been swimming, Tim—but it wasn't like the old times. Why did you do it, man? All the accidents."

Tim's eyes glittered hard and cold. "*I* should have been running the camp, not that pencil-pusher," he growled, jerking his head in Harry's direction. "When Dad died, Uncle Harry just took over. He stole what was mine. He stole my *life* away from me!"

Jack shook his head sadly. "Harry didn't steal anything, Tim. He was your father's partner. And down the road, the whole company would have been all yours."

"You don't understand," Tim said. "I can't wait that long. Time is running out. Soon there won't *be* any more independent logging companies. Loggers are already on the endangered species list." He sounded very bitter. Suddenly a look of deep sadness filled his face. "I didn't mean for anyone to get hurt."

"But they did, Tim. We both could have been killed today, setting those chokes."

"We weren't *supposed* to be working as choke setters, remember? Harry switched the work assignments," Tim said. He hung his head and stared at the floor. When he looked up, his mood had changed again. "Do you know why I wanted *you* to help us find out who was sabotaging the camp?" Now Tim's face wore an expression of hate and scorn.

"No."

"Because I knew that you'd never suspect me. You still see me as I was in high school," sneered Tim.

Jack didn't say anything. Tim was right. He had wondered about Tim's mood swings, but he'd never suspected him for a minute.

"Who did you suspect was doing it, Jack?" asked Tim.

"Lou Williams. I saw him leaving Bowers' Lodge the other night. I thought he must be working with the protesters."

Tim snickered. "Lou has a girlfriend who works as a pastry chef over at the lodge. He goes over there to see her."

"Yeah, he told me that tonight," said Jack. He glanced over at the cook, who sat talking quietly with Ron Bueller.

Tim laughed, then motioned for Jack to come closer. "You've got to watch out for John Bowers and those tree-huggers, Jack. *They* are the dangerous ones," warned Tim, his eyes wide with fear. Then suddenly he stood up and started yelling. "They're *coming!* The tree-huggers are coming to get us. I've got to warn Dad!"

Harry and the sheriff rushed over to him. Reaching out, Harry put his hand on Tim's shoulder and tried to calm him down. "No one's going to get us, Tim. John Bowers can file as many petitions with the state as he wants—but he won't win. And the protesters can demonstrate until they're blue in the face. They won't stop us."

Roughly, Tim pushed the older man's hand away. Jack saw the concern in Harry's eyes as he looked at his nephew. Tim clearly needed help. Whatever it took, Harry would get it for him.

Jack followed Tim and Harry to the patrol car. A wave of sadness rolled over him as he watched them drive away. Glancing up at the mountain, Jack saw the giant Douglas firs glistening fresh and clean in the morning air. He heard the word *Timber!* echo across the valley.